My Culture

and the

Environment

MY CULTURE
and the
ENVIRONMENT

DR. ALHASSAN NDEKUGRI

Library of Congress Control Number: 2019919489

PAPERBACK: 978-1-951461-76-8
EBOOK: 978-1-951461-77-5

Ordering Information:

For orders and inquiries, please contact:
1-888-404-1388
www.goldtouchpress.com
book.orders@goldtouchpress.com

Printed in the United States of America

TABLE OF CONTENTS

My culture and the environment

By

ALHASSAN NDEKUGRI

....

....

....

....

....

....

....

....

....

....

....

....

....

....

....

My life has been full of thoughts of the environment and the future it has on the world.

A world of less pollution is a World of good health and a world of good wealth, actions and in actions about the environment has millions of questions to ask and of course millions of solutions. But how does Culture affect the environment? My culture, your culture and our culture have pros and cons depending on how you view it from a perspective. Cultural dynamics or cultural conservatism have been on the two side of the coin. How do we conserve culture? And how does it affect the environment in which we leave in? In the ancient culture everything from the clothes we wear, to the bowl in which we eat and to the shoes we wear were made from trees and plants around us. I still remember the calabash, the clay pot, the clay bowl, the stirrer, the and the Bamboo sticks all were biodegradable and very friendly to the environment, in fact one could dis integrate them within a matter of minutes and they form part of the soil saving the world cost of recycling and less pollution of course. In the ancient culture, many were bathed from the calabash, women used the calabash as bras, we also used the calabash to harvest produce, store food, prepare local dish and even use it as take away for local snacks, we used the calabash to produce music and we also trade calabash for money. Production of calabash was as simple as sowing the seed and taking care of the geminated plant to grow, the leaves of the plants covers the entire space making it look green and preventing the land from being heated and as a result, no erosion or washing of the top-most part of the soil. The calabash protected most soil for years while at the same time, used for so many artifacts including design, roofing of local houses serving as wind breaks and for beautification purposes. Today, many people have forgotten of the famous calabash because plastics have substituted the calabash, the clay pot and wooded stirrer have almost gone plastic. Whiles we are happy of this substitution, it is also the contributory factor of global warming that the human had faced today, and the future is uncertain with the increasing dominance of plastics all over the world. A world of the calabash, the clay pot, and the Bamboo will be a sustainable one with less cost to degrade them and more certain of what they contribute to the environment. A friend last said to me, hi friend, I see that you are worried about the environment and the future of all the living around the world, you have been emphasizing on the protection of the environment, but don't you think we are in the modern world? Doing all things in a modern way? The modern world is all about fashion, think of the flashy laptop, the flashy phone, the flashy wrist watches, the flashy hair breads, the flashy pens, the flashy airplane, cars, and all the flashy artifacts are made from plastics and the world had seen happiness through these flashy materials why then complain about the earth? And I said well, whiles I agree with you for all the enjoyment we had with the flashy material, my science professor told me when I was in the high school that it takes hundreds of years to disintegrate plastics and the earth will never be peaceful with plastic pollution and that was the reason for my worry. Do you share with my worry? If so, then hi five! Our worries are that water bodies would be polluted beyond good for drinking and even if you drink, your will be full of traces of plastics making us sick daily. Do you want to be bed ridden because of drinking polluted water? No country wants to reduce its productivity because the youth and women are mostly the victims of sickness and diseases, ironically, they are also the most productive age group, no wonder Countries that record high prevalence of disease outbreak if not well manage keep on becoming poorer and poorer! Think of cholera outbreak that is caused by dirt, What of the cerebrospinal meningitis that is caused by an intense heat that takes hundreds of the lives around the world? This calls for everyone to be worried right?

GOOD CULTURE AND THE CONSERVATION OF WETLANDS

About twenty years ago, there were a lot of happiness in my village, in fact just about three meters away from my house, the was water stored in the valley, in this water, you could find the following creatures: fish, frogs, turtles, snakes, alligators, crocodiles, the swimming birds, water lily and a host of other beautiful flowers making the whole place glamorous and so attractive. At that time, there were little or no plastic materials, so we use to buy most of our snacks in paper made bag and cold water were from the earthenware pot. As a result of these biodegradable materials, the environment was safe because most of these materials that found their way into the water bodies were able to disintegrate easily. I still remember that most of my village people use that water for many purposes including but not limited to bathing, building houses, watering plants, growing crops and raring animals. The gardeners near that water bodies used to cultivate a lot of vegetables such as the Okra, the tomato, Onions, Lettuce, Cabbage, Carrots, Pepper, garden egg, thereby supplying the whole village and beyond a happy organic food for consumption. I still remember the busy nature of that wonder village with children learning to build using the mud and the plenty of sand around, and others happily playing soccer, Ampee, hide and seek on the sand. The stored water at that time provided the people not only several source of food but also it had provided the people the opportunity to have a good teamwork spirit, unity, care for one another and sense of belongings, creating an excellent rapport for peaceful co-existence. After about five years later, with the emergence of plastics that we taught was going to make life comfortable and easier, we rather realized a lot of calamities in the village. Hmm., why are the people in my village unhappy now? You know what? My village wetland started disappearing…uh? As I read to you somebody, my village water body had finally disappeared. It is very evident that a stranger or those children born after the mighty village wetlands if not through stories and folktales, these children will never realize that there was a wetland in their village. The place looks dry, dusty and disappointed. Animals' passes through the valley searching for nonexistent water to quince their thirst, there are no more beautiful flowers for children to play with, and one could see a mirage on the spotted valley on a very strong sunshine day. I still remember an attempt by my village people to drill a hole on the valley for water and had gone more than six feet deep without sign of water. So, where has the water gone? May be the plastics had drunk all the water? Hmm, what a real calamity? What a disappointment? What a disadvantage of the plastic?

RIVER GODS OR THE CARELESSNESS OF HUMAN

The importance of water in my village became apparent when the mighty water body started drying up, At the time the water was disappearing or decreasing in volume and decreasing in size in the number of creatures, many people had attributed it to the anger of the village gods for lack of sacrifice. My village people made several attempts to save the water body that unified the whole village and fed everyone but through the wrong methods. Aah? But that was the culture of the people, to make consultations with the gods to find a solution to pressing problem. What could have been the main cause of the drying of this savior wetland at that time? Your guess could be as good as mine; the introduction of plastic materials was patronized by the people to carry water. Most at times, these plastics that wear out into the water body were non-biodegradable and as a result, were polluting the water source while at the same time, blocking the source of water. Most of the creatures such as the fish, the turtles, the alligator, and all the birds migrated to an unknown location leaving the wonder village very dry, disserted and disappointed.

Oh my God, what a dilemma! Is my culture friendly? Well my culture was friendly, but my village adopted a culture they never know well about. For instance, at the time where the people used materials made from plants, these were all biodegradable and did not serve as a danger to the water bodies but with the introduction of the so called portable and dependable plastics were not well managed and serve as a danger that wipe out the water and the whole creatures leaving the village so dry. Have you also experienced such a problem in your village, town or city? What were the feelings of the people, what were the feelings of your family? What will you do differently to save your wonder village, town or city? Do the people in your village, town or city took the same method employed in my village to avert any calamity? Did they succeed or failed with that methodology? Oh mine, I said to myself that there was the need to understand the culture around the world. The plastic cultures., the calabash culture, the clay pot culture, the culture of conserving, the culture of maintenance and the educational culture of knowing oneself and where you came from and stopping the culture of blind copying. Throwing your culture could have a consequence such as the one that occurred in my wonder village. Maybe I need to educate my people about differences in culture, differences in technology and differences in maintenance culture around the world. Financially, we are different to take up environmental issues, technologically we are different in terms of application to solve a problem but what we have in common is paying attention to our environment, and seeing your environment as the place that support your life, your family and the world.

"What we should understand is that there are no climate changes, but rather the activities of man that causes the climate to change and we must act responsibly to reverse this phenomenon"

EDUCATION AND CULTURAL DYNAMICS

Education is tool for national development, the world twenty years today will not be the same as the world twenty years to come because of several factors including but not limited to technology, migration, weather, and the way we think as humans. The evolution of technology has significantly changed the culture around the world; in the way we eat, the way we drink, the way we talk, the way we travel, the way we sleep, the way we sit and the way we do things around us signifies the cultural dynamics. The robotic world will change my culture, your culture and our culture in the way we work, the way enemies fight among themselves and the way lovers loves themselves. In short, call it the robotic culture is the culture where everything will be controlled by robots in the home to clean the environment, in the hospital to perform surgery, at the work place to take attendance, do cashier work, play managerial role, production and in cars to self-drive. That is the culture we are migrating into. May be my village had embraced a culture they were not aware of the consequence where now there is no water to cultivate their vegetables and fed the water creature. I wonder the way forward for generations to come how exactly the world of 2099 will look like. If you are predicting a robotic world, you may be right. The world of the robot is going to be the most powerful one but if care is not put in place the robot will control us such that it may take over 1,000 years before we regain our freedom. Is this statement funny? Then be on the lookout…, in my village, the migration of birds, turtles, snakes, crocodiles, alligators, and many other creatures do not only vanish from their habitats but today what do see around the world? Villages, towns and cities are heating up, there is unpredictable rain fall, wildfires have taken out the love of our environment and today the environment is annoyed with us.

MISTRUST OF HUMANS AND CULTURAL DYNAMICS

Who controls the world? Humans or nature...? In the creation of the world, control has been in the mouth of many people. Who control in terms of gender? Who controls in terms of race, who controls in terms of riches and who controls in terms of cultural heritages? Control has led to mistrust of humans since the beginning of creation because there is limitation in the process of control such that so many questions are being ask such as… why are some people oppressively controlled? Why are others being caged? And freedom suppressed. Luck of trust can be contributed to so many factors including racial divide, religious divide and even geographical divide and can be seen clearly at the workplace, in restaurants, in schools, and even at the place of worship where there is pretense. But how does mistrust affect us and the environment in which we live in? People should be trusted for the work they do, for instance if you are paid to take care of the trees, the water bodies, and the animals then that trust should be upheld in a highest esteem. Reports all over the world are that people mined natural resources without permission, people fell down trees without permission and people hunt at the wrong time, fishermen fish on the water at the wrong time resulting in catching the younger fishes instead of the grown up ones. These reports generates questions of mistrust on the part of those paid to perform their duties, the indiscriminate felling of trees without replacement could have an effect on the environment, such as inadequate rain fall, desertification and luck of rain fall leads to no water in the rivers, ponds and other places such as the streams and canals…..? As a result, the consequential effects are that no water for animals to drink, no water to grow other plants and water for the rural folks who depend largely on these water bodies to grow their food plants such as the onion, the lettuce, the water melon, the red radish, egg plant, the sweet potatoes, the black eye beans, the okra, the yams, the tomatoes, the sweet and hot pepper. Mistrust even affects us in the food that we eat daily, the stories that we tell and the report that we write in our schools, workplace, the mosque, in the church, in our businesses and all other places of importance.

THE PROJECTILE CULTURE, HOW IT STOLE MY LOVE

Cultural adoption has been part of humanity for so many years, for instance, the religious culture where a religion have been adopted by a group of people in a community, a town, a city or a country. But have you ever thought of the gun culture that humanity have adopted around the world that have destroyed us? The gun according the layman definition is a machine that propels projectiles aimed at a direction. The gun could be used for hunting game, defense etc. So many years ago, the gun was a popular name associated with the hunter, the army, and the police, but of late, the gun has become a common name where even a two year old play with it, as a result, instead of the gun being use for defense, it has become a very distractive projectile instead of a defensive one. Hmm, the gun stole my love, your love, and our love. Every day, we hear of the destructions caused by the gun, the shooting spree in the homes, our schools, the church, the Mosque, the airport, the restaurants, the shopping mall, and the entertainment centers around the world, in some parts of the world, people only hear of gun shorts when they are at war but in other parts of the world, shooting a gun is fun and killing is a fun too. Oh! what a sad story to say? Why are people adopting a culture that is offensive, destructive and unfriendly to the lives of others? When can we as people adopt a friendly culture that is free of depression, isolation, and alienation of families? Why wouldn't people adopt a culture that brings families together? Bring harmonization of religion for the peace of the world? Projectiles do not only destroy people but also destroy the environment and all the beauty that comes with it, the gun idea has never been of a good thinking to some people as a result of that, the idea has lead to a development of a more sophisticated projectiles such as the submarine missiles, the short, medium and long range missiles that has the highest potential of destroying the beautiful environment besides, the destruction of the human population. Why are world leaders competing in the production of weapons of mass destruction and refusing to collaborate to reduce the increasing nature of climate change? To some leaders, climate change is a hoax whiles war is real. Lost of focus, direction and commitment to ensure the safety of the environment and its people around the world is making us noxious, tasty and lost!

....

....

....

....

....

....

....

....

....

....

....

....

....

....

....

....

DISCRIMINATION AGAINST HUMANS AFFECTS THE ENVIRONMENT

Discriminations come in so many forms; base on gender, color, religion, geographical location and the list goes on and on. Human discrimination has a very serious repercussions, for instance, if you discriminate against a fellow human and where he or she lives, you are directly discriminating against the environment. For instance, people who are normally discriminated on do not suffer alone, but they suffer with their animals, trees and all the plans located on the environment. In some parts of the world, damping is common because some people think that it is the good place to throw their expired products. This is simply an environmental discrimination, the people in that environment may be deceived to think that it is a help to make their life better, but the long run consequence of that damping cannot be measured, and the people suffer with little or no help. If the help comes it is always too late when the harm has already been worsened. If you hate my environment, you directly hated me, if you like me, then respect my little environment by helping to keep it clean, and you can only do this by preventing dumping. Your dumping is causing my little fishes to die in the sea, making our birds, lions, elephants, the giraffe, the turtles, the peacocks, the monkey, the chimpanzee, the zebra, the buffalo, not forgetting of the donkey, the horse, the sheep, the goat and all the beautiful animals to migrate leaving our environment very frustrated, very angry, and very disappointed, please live my environment alone. My environment is part of the world's environment, why make yours clean and try to make mine dirty? See my environment as equally important, respect the people who lives in that environment. Let the animals feel safe, help to conserve the antelope, the water bucks the baboons, the bunny, the millipedes, and the ox. Work with your family and friends to protect the environment, conserve the wetlands, the ponds, the river, the Ocean, the Sea and your community. If you are damping in my environment, then teach me how to clean the mess may be? Some people should also learn how to say no to damping, no is not crime but a message that something is not right, unacceptable and wrong that needs to be corrected. No should not be a way of vengeance but just of correcting the ills and helping to safe my little corner and your cleanest city.

....

....

....

....

....

THE SEA LIFE AND THE BEAUTY OF THE PEOPLE

Have you ever wondered how it is to visit the sea and enjoy the beautiful environment of the sea? Try it and you will never forget in your lifetime you leaved on earth. They are many rivers around the globe, and they contribute meaningfully in our lives, think of water transportation where goods are carried from one place to the other. What of the pleasure of sea navigation, think of Cancun of Mexico, a travel to the Bahamas, the Caribbean, do you remember Hawaii and the beautiful environment? What of the salt we get from the sea especially from Ghana along the coast? What of the river Nile; one of the longest in the world that stretches with a distance assumed to be over 1000kilometers or 620 miles. There is beauty in that river; I once had the opportunity to visit the river Nile with a ride on the canoe, and the African queen. Having the full view of the river in all perspective, observing the river banks; enjoying the little holes created by the birds, the Hypos displaying on the water, the crocodiles swimming across in styles, the alligators exhibiting their skills, observing the fly of the birds in a certain styles make people forget of their stress, the water waves were beautifully displayed and observing the nature of the river create memories. A trip to the Murchison falls also known as the Kabalega falls usually starts with the African Queen, a bigger canoe used to transport tourist along the river to their destinations. Oh what a wonder island on the river Nile?, very interesting to shop on the Island, you have to be prepared and make sure that you carry enough money to shop at the river Nile Island where products sold there may be as twice as products sold off the river because you get to see the source of the river Nile where one can stand with confidence and take a selfie to show the world. This is the beauty of the environment that we discussed about; this is the reason why it is good to discard discrimination against the environment. Millions of people visit the river Nile and many other rivers around the world for entertainment, for educational purposes, for healing, for business and for tourism. Whiles you have the opportunity to visit all these important rivers, create the opportunity for others to do same by conserving them; preventing river pollution, preventing damping that leads to river blockage, creating a good environment for the crocodile, the hypos, and the alligator so that they can continuously display to entertain us any time we revisit the rivers.

THE LIFE OF THE LION AND HAPPINESS OF THE WORLD

The lion is the most powerful animal on earth; even my little daughters once remembered that the lion is the king of the jungle. There are currently scares lions on earth, this means that the lion is becoming an endangered spice and if care is not taken, our future children may only hear of the lion but will not have the opportunity to see it physically except for a picture. Do you remember the dinosaur? My children, your children and our children want to see the dinosaur physically but are disappointed because the dinosaur is an extinct animal. My experience with a visit to the Ugandan game reserve indicated that the population of the lion keeps decreasing and decreasing. A funny question was thrown to one of the professional and experienced game guard's drivers. Question, why are the lions known as the king of the jungle decreasing in their numbers?

Answer, the female lion takes between 105 to 110 days to give birth to the young one, also, the lion is the most hatred animal in the jungle because of its bullying nature. As a result, any time the parent mistakenly leaves the young one to look for food; other animals also prey on them, thereby reducing the population of lions in the jungle. Isn't this interesting about how other animals hate the progress of the lion? Well the king of the jungle does the same to other animals and may be a payback time right? Also, out of fear and the wickedness of human, the lion is always the target by hunters any time the two came face to face for fear of reprisal attach, thereby also reducing the population of the lion. As a result, the lion has so many enemies, including the human, fellow animals, bush fire, aging, and deforestation. But the lion can be the friendliest animal when treated with care. It can be used as a pet and even most people like to associate their product with the strength of the lion to depict product durability and long-lasting ability and product quality. As you may know, product durability is what drives demand for it and the power of the product to cure is of paramount importance, for that reason, companies used the lion, and you may hear names such as Leopard ointment or lion power. These brand names are all testimonies for the powerful nature of the king of the jungle. Even in most communities around the world where people practice the traditional religion, the bone of the lion is used to bathe newborn boys. Can anyone guess the reason for mixing the bone of the lion to bathe boys? If your guess was to make the boys grow stronger like the lion then you may be right. Even today, it is believed that men fight in time of war and as a result, there is the need to fortify men physically, spiritually, psychologically and mentally to stand the test of time in times of war. Demand for the bones of the lion has led to the discriminate hunting of the of the lion in Africa, Asia, the Americas, Europe and many parts of the world hence decreasing the population of the lion globally. Psychologically, people get heals quickly with the use of these products. Yet these companies seldom contribute a penny to care for the lion to live longer. If the lion is really the king of the jungle, then we will lose the king one day to extinction due to our own wickedness. Lets us help to prolong the life of the lion so that we can have the king of the jungle and the king of the home, it is very interesting to visit the king of the jungle in their natural home, spending days, hours and every minute just to catch a glimpse of it. Exploring in the forest, on top of tall trees, and rocks… ust to hear the word here comes the lion. Unlike any other animal in the jungle, the lion is the most respected animal to trek at. But be very careful in trekking the king of the jungle because it is a wild animal and may not be your friend sometimes; the lion may be hungry or angry and as a result can transfer it anger and hunger on you. Give a distance when you are in the jungle, be safe in your movement and make sure to be with expects such as the jungle tour guard. Never play a fool with the king Bobo of the jungle. In Uganda, Kenya, Tanzania, Rwanda and other African countries as well as Asian Countries where the lion can be seen in the wild, make sure to handle your children with care, handle your family with care so that you do not have a bad vacation as it happened in the past. The speed of the lion is unmatched and never be a victim of trying to race with the king, for you will always be the loser!!

THE RHINO AND THE ENRICHMENT OF OUR CULTURE

The Rhinos contribute a lot to the environment and cultural heritage of a society. Many people around the world are talking about the Rhino now and then; Tourist spend a lot of money to travel both far and near to catch the glimpse of the Rhino. There are two main types of Rhinos; the black and the white Rhinos are mostly found in Africa, as heavy as the Rhino may be, it can run as fast more than the human, as a result, care should be taken trekking the Rhino. Rhinos in their natural home can be very beautiful especially when it is poised for picture, when trekking the Rhino in their natural home, make sure there are absolute silence because they are very sensitive to noise and you may not get the full view of the Rhino if the environment is very noisy. According to the tour guard of the endangered species, the Rhino can run very faster than the human does, and we need to keep a distance to prevent the wrath of it if the Rhino senses danger. In spite of the fact that Rhinos contribute very significantly both economically and culturally for the benefit of society, unfortunately, human are not contributing enough for the survival of the beautiful Rhinos in Africa and in many parts of the world, and this has led to the reduction in numbers of the Rhinos. It is believed that the horns of the Rhino are highly marketable in some parts of the world and are used for medicinal purposes and expensive gift. For this reason, people hunt for the tusk and horn of the Rhino by indiscriminately killing them just to take their task and the whole body is left to rot. To protect the beautiful Rhino and contributing to their growth let's stop our selfish desire of the little amount of money through the sales of the tusk of the Rhino and think of the beautiful body that is abandoned to rot forever.

GOOD CULTURE OF THE GIRAFFE

The giraffe is one of an interesting animal to watch at the game reserve, while they may be a scientific reason why the giraffe has a long neck, the traditional people speculates that the giraffe like to live in the savanna land where the only source of its food are the tall trees that it graces on, as a result, the giraffe must adapt to its natural environment by growing tall legs and neck to be able to reach the high tree for food thereby developing a long neck. Whether this idea is back by science or not is not the issue, what is important is that when people travel to the game reserve, they want to enjoy the beauty of the giraffe in their natural, watching them grace the tall trees and poising for a picture that create happiness and helps to reduce stress of the individual, watching them run creates amusement and people are willing to pay huge sums of money to visit the giraffe so they can tell stories to their love one. While some giraffe has red spots, other giraffes have black spots; tour guards speculate that the black spot giraffe indicates aging of the animal whiles the red spot giraffes means that the giraffe is still young.

SAFE THE ELEPHANT TO PROMOTE CULTURE

The elephant is one of the biggest mammals on earth, they are mostly found in Africa and Asian countries. The elephant is a very friendly animal, when it is domesticated, people can ride on its back for pleasure, even in the game reserve, birds found a source of happiness by riding on the back of the elephant. As big as the elephant is it can be controlled by the little bumble bee such that they can cry the whole day and breaking down trees to safe itself from the trauma of the small but troublesome bumble bee, isn't this so funny and interesting? Observing the ear of the elephant moves and flaps can be entertaining. Unfortunately, the elephants face a lot of challenges including but limited to the bumming ivory market in most part of the world including Asia, the premature death of the young ones through wildfire and the activities of hunters can be very disturbing to the very survival of the elephant. Instead of killing the elephant for their tusk to sell and make a small amount of money, there should be a campaign to save the elephant. "May be safe the elephant now" could be powerful message to send to the world. A lot can be done to learn from the successful elephant with a very big and heavy body but does not easily sink in the mud; the elephant can be trained to carry out rescue missions in time of danger such as flooding. The elephant can be as intelligent as the human, humans are not the only creatures that create a barrier or stoppage, but the elephant does the same to show their superiority over humanity when you visit these elephants in their natural home. The friendly nature of the elephants makes it able to walk with birds on top of its back to show that thought the elephant is strong and destructive sometimes, it can tolerate other animals including the bird. Below shows the power of the elegant elephant and the superiority it has by creating a no way through when the writer visited them in the Ugandan game reserve. They showed power in the display of their bodies including their tusk which serves as a controversy through which the elephant population is reduced by the selfish individuals around the world.

In many parts of the world, there are numerous personnel serving as a guard in the game reserve because of the rate at which predators are preying on these animals. But this continuous guidance will not stop the activities of humans who see the elephant Ivory as a source of income. However, education can send a powerful message to the world letting people know that conserving the population of elephant will provide a contiguous employment for a larger number of people as compared to the very few greedy people who kill the elephant just for the Ivory. Joint hands to fight for the survival of the elephant, the Lion, the Giraffe, the Rhino, the Crocodile, the Alligator, not forgetting of the Monkey, the water buck, the bush pig…..to make the world an un-regrettable place for the growing population.

TREKKING THE CHIMPANZEE IN THEIR NATURAL HOME

The Chimpanzee is one of the humans like animal found in the forest especially on tall trees during the daytime and at night as a result, it becomes very challenging at times come face to face with them. Just like many other animals that are becoming very extinct, the Chimpanzee is increasingly being one of them. It is believed that the Chimpanzee can live up to 62 years when in captivity but 40-50 years when in the wild. Have you ever visited the Chimpanzee in the zoo or in the wild? If you do, you will remember that it is very challenging trekking it in their natural home, however, the challenge comes with a joy when you finally spot them on a branch high on top of a tall tree, with so many people running and falling just to catch a glimpse of it. What of if finally, the Chimpanzee decides to descend from the high spotted branch to the ground with its majestic walk? You will like the combination of the green leaves and the dry branches that makes you wants to run more towards it for a full view. I remember that trekking the Chimpanzee require time, patience, and energy to walk for a long time while both high in the rain fall forest and, on the ground, to find a good path to walk through the tick and bushy forest. It is also required that you wear the right footwear such as the rain boot and dress appropriately for the journey mostly in the rain forest. I remember that in Uganda, it takes about 15minutes to 30minutes walk with the tour guard to be able to spot the much-awaited Chimps as it is normally called. The tour guard serves as the leader, giving all instructions including but not limited signs of spotting a Chimp. These leaders also have corresponding leaders with handheld radios; Chimps are monitored by the lead tour guards throughout the day and communicates to visiting leaders as the direction to follow for a successful trekking. We were told not to hold the chimps nor feed them at their natural home instead gives a distance in order not to be infested with diseases since some of them have communicable ones. Because of the high nature of the trees, be prepared to have neck crams the following day because of the continuous upwards looking to spot the Chimps, it also involves a lengthy walk with less communications except the tour guard giving instructions. Trekking the Chimpanzee creates memories, reduces boring nature of the body when you decide to visit the Chimpanzee in their natural home. Be prepared to have a lot of fall because of the slippery nature of the forest... including small sink holes, wild prey thorns I can still remember how to imitate how the champs cry...wo- wooo, wo-wooo, wo-wooo were some of the sounds made by the champs to locate one another in the forest. Trekking the champs also gives the opportunity to learn the culture of others by appreciating their way of life through the continuous interactions and sharing of ideas. What makes the world a beautiful place is not just the beauty of the people, but the beauty of the environment, including the water bodies, the trees, the animals the birds, the skies, the clouds, the roads, the houses for that matter the weather, and the dance of the people makes a beautiful world.

GLOBAL WARMING OR CLIMATE CHANGE AND THE FUTURE OF THE SHREDDING WORLD

When I was a student growing up, I learned of the ozone layer, I was told that there was a hole in the Ozone layer that has a consequence on my future. My question was how can a hole that is very far away from me affect my life in years to come? My science teacher at that time said that the earth was heating up or warming due to Chlorofluorocarbons and rise of these heat or hot gases will affect us in so many ways; including the dying of plants, dying of most valued animals including but not limited to the lion; the king of the jungle, the elephant, the buffalo, the zebra, the dear, the Chimpanzee, the monkey, not forgetting of the crocodile, the alligator, the turtles, the birds such as the peacock, the eagle, sparrow, the crow, the cattle egret, the beetle eater, and many more other animals. He said the wetland and other water bodies will also dry up where animals will scramble for non-existent water and humans will pay for high price for drinking water and that humans will therefore remember the word global warming. Several efforts have been made about curbing global warming, but all approaches may not realize a holistic solution if the mindset of the individual remain the same. Technological advancement has solved so many problems around the world whiles at the same time have also created so many problems around the globe. Do you remember some ugly side of global warming in your life? If not, think of the desertification in most part of the world… Most Countries today are covered by some form of desert, making it difficult for trees to grow or for cultivation purpose. Also, lack of trees increases the intensity of heat and unbearable environmental conditions and human suffering. Wait a minute, have you thought of the increasing nature of hurricanes? Tornadoes? and tsunamis around the world? The intensity of these hurricanes and tornadoes have generated their own fearful names to remember; mention hurricane Harvey and people will start to scream because of the havoc it had caused to the good people of Houston with about 125 billion lost and more than 60 deaths. Is this not a bad memory? What of hurricane Maria in the Dominica and Puerto Rico causing more than 3,000 deaths and millions of people displaced? The business that were lost and the hope of the people dismantled at that time were worse in history. Think of Hurricane Katrina that also caused havoc to central Florida to the Eastern Taxes? Are these not disturbing occurrences? What of Lee County in Alabama? Tornadoes can strike with little warning! People need help in times of disaster, it makes sense for a timely support for fellow brothers and sisters to find a place to sleep, water to drink, food to eat not forgetting the lost ones, consoling words are needed to heal families emotionally. Do you also remember the Indonesian tsunami? What of the Japanese Earthquake? I still remember the outbreak of the deadly Ebola virus in Liberia, Editorial Guinea and sierra Leon that swept people untimely and the pain it had caused to families, friends and the world at large. What of the Cyclone Idai in Zimbabwe, Mozambique and Malawi that killed over 700 people and left many homeless? With many people needing water, food, medicine and shelter, many have also been reported missing and many families alienated, the psychological trauma and the emotional pain will last for years. Will it be out of place to say that humans are our own enemies in our own world if we refused to come together to combat climate change and the negative repercussions it has on us in this planet?

"THE POLLUTER PAY PRINCIPLE" THEN AND NOW

There is supposed to be happiness living in an environment the world over, such as clean air to breath, clean water to drink, and good health to create wealth. But today, some people are sick because there is no clean air for them to breadth, there is no clean water for them to drink and people are not wealthy because they are not healthy. Is the polluter pay principle creating good health for all or good wealth for a few people? What was the main objective of the polluter pay principle? Will it be out of place to say that the polluter pay principle has created more wealth for the rich and suffering for the poor? These are questions that need answers because there is a school of thought that if I can pay to pollute the environment, and then I have the right to pollute the environment the more. And those who cannot pay to go to the hospital when the environment is polluted suffer the more for no fault of theirs. Where are the environmentalists? Where are the environmental regulators? What will be the future of the world? What is the future of the human race, the elephant, squirrel, the zebra, the crocodile, turtles, Rhino, the giraffe, the panda, the silk worm, the turkey, the fish, the sea lion, the snake, the bats, the spider, Raccoon, and the whale? Rivers are chocked because of pollution, the gutters are chocked because of pollution, there is flooding pandemic because people care less for the environment and the environment "seems" to be punishing us. People of this World, please rise and be vigilant to protect the environment and not political vigilantism, the environment needs care, the environment needs protection, the environment needs planning to be sustainable, and be successful. Let your culture reflects positively on the environment, a culture that care for the environment is a culture worthy of emulation, my culture, your culture and our culture should not wait for the polluter pay principle to act but a holistic action for life.

THE CULTURE OF GREEN FINANCE AND THE ENVIRONMENT

A holistic fight is needed to succeed in the fight of global warming or climate change; green finance shows care and care means love for all, green finance should bring into light the friendly behavior of business and finance. It is true that business and finance hold the world with the responsible use of science and technology to create product and services for our benefit. Every year government around the world has put aside millions and billions of dollars to fight climate change but when are we achieving the results? Are some of the failures to meet a target due to leadership failure, carelessness, corruption or negligence? If so where are the moral decadence, the consciousness of the mind, the willingness of the body and the togetherness of the world? Where is the unity, the common goal, the objective? Words or action?, theory or practice?, prevention or cure?, politics as usual or real?, prevent the world from its shredding nature, from its deterioration and from its depletion of the outer layer, support the dream of the environment and the subsequent dream of the world. Our dream of success is meaningless if there is no link to the dream of the environment, let's dream holistically. I was approached by a friend with a question that keeps me searching for answers; do you like to write on paper, he asked, and do you like to take your receipt from the cashier after transaction? Will you prefer more paper use or less paper usage? These were the tough questions. My search and findings had the following: The papers and books we write on are all made from plants, the receipts and all the invoices are from plants. So, the analysis is that; how many trees are fell daily to produce books, invoices and receipts around the world? How many trees are replaced daily if so how many years does it take to grow a tree to replace those cut for domestic use such as the books, the receipts, the invoice, the boxes for packing, for constructions in the housing industry, the hospitals, the factories, in the homes for ceilings and many more. What of the free-range systems in many parts of the world where animals can grace, some trees are destroyed by these animals and other weather conditions. What of the destructions caused by wildfire and flooding? Who replaces all those trees? No wonder the desertification is catching up with the world. The culture of replanting,… may be going paperless in terms of issuing of receipts and invoices to reduce the felling of trees to produce papers, books and other related paper usage?....teaching using online resources, encouraging electronic books usage instead of hard copies are but a few of the efforts to adopt

CARELESS CULTURE, WILDFIRE AND THE ENVIRONMENT

Careless of one person could lead to the destruction of the world, my tears run down to hear about the wildfires around the world and the destructions it had caused, the pain that people have endured, the lost of love ones and properties. In Africa, Asia, The Americas, the Europe, the Middle East and all other parts of world, wild fire does not only cause the pain to humans, but also had caused the migration of many animals running for their lives, destruction of food and farm land had led to hunger and the migration of humans causing the dynamics of culture, politics and finance. Have you heard about the wildfire in California? Hmmm…., so sad to say that houses were reduced to ashes, humans to charcoal and the beautiful environment turned ugly. Thousands got displaced and many went missing. Stand up to protect the environment and safe your family, stand up to protect the environment and save your country, stand up to protect the environment and save the world, stand up with California to reduce the pain inflicted to families, friends, society and the state. Stand up to save the animals including the dog, the cat, the goat, the sheep, the bird, the buffalo, the lion, the zebra, the bee, the raccoon, and the antelope, stand up to protect the green leaves to put a smile in the face of the disappointed, stand up to protect and save the atmosphere, stand up and give meaning to the clean air fight, stand up and help to protect the poor and all those who cannot afford for high cost of health care due to environmental factors, such as the rising temperatures, help to save the world and save a life. My life, your life and our lives are dependent on the environment; do not be deceived to think that you can fly to the sky, the moon, and all other planet because you will land back on earth which widely is our home of abode.

I still remember fresh in my mind the effort taken by the many men and women in uniform to control wildfire around the world, California inclusive, so many of them lost their lives in trying to protect the environment, human lives and properties. Many of them flying on air and on land, the distress calls for help to safety, the distress calls for help during the day, during the night, whiles some were lucky and got help, others were unlucky and got over powered by the blazing fire, others got chocked by the heavy smock. These smocks could be seen high in the air like dark clouds, we could see on television how animals were rescued including the rat, the dog, the squirrel, the birds, the turtles the lizard and the monkey. Oh, what a sad story? The many aircrafts flying over the blazing fire at an altitude but could not easily succeed in putting of the fire because it was so strong and wide, but sometimes, calamities happens at a time where there is little help, for instance at the time of wild fire in California, there was little or no rain to complement the effort of the men and women in uniform. Let us protect our environment for a continuous rain; a one-day rain could have saved the lives of many that would take months of humans to fight. What is your contribution to ensuring the safety of the environment? Report suspicious and potential fire, for instance, electric wire sparks, people smoking and throwing away their cigarette butts, people looking for bush meat may be some of the causes to the destruction of the environment and the lost of many lives. Humans may be able to discriminate against one and another based on race, gender, religion and color but wildfire has no discrimination, and the destruction is limitless. For this reason, are you ready? And Are we ready? To hold hands and say enough is enough to the destruction of the environment, are we ready to put aside the racism, the segregation, and nepotism and collectively fight for the safety of the world, the environment and the better living of humans?

HOW LOCAL CULTURE HELPS IN PROTECTING THE ENVIRONMENT

In Many parts of the world, where people believe in deities, Mountains, Rivers, Rocks and special trees serve as shrine, any attempt to cut down those special trees are met with punishment from the village gods. Certain rivers are forbidden from fishing at certain time of the year and certain Rocks are also forbidden to be harvested. These believe had helped to protect the environment in the past. There were no strong legal systems to punish perpetrators of the destruction of the environment, however, for the fear of the river god, the tree god, the Rock god and the Mountain god, people acted just right. It was believed that any disobedience was met with several calamities such prolong sickness and even death. Wonderful culture isn't it? But wait a minute for more cultural story, do not eat with your left hand is also part of some culture, the right hand is supreme in some culture where you have to only great with the right hand, eat with the right hand and collect good things with the right hand and pick up things that are bad with left hand. The left hand only supports the right hand in greeting, lifting, drinking, and giving, pointing to somebody with the left hand is seen as an offense in some culture and requires an apology. What about writing using the right hand? Have you ever reason why some animals are extinct? In some parts of the world, hunting and killing certain wild animals are prestigious and the killing of such animals are praised in society as a strong person and given some concoctions for protection against the bad spirits of the killed animals. The killer of the wild animals dresses in a certain way to announce his strength and power of a distinct power such as wearing the horns of the animal, wearing the skin of the animal and handling a bow and arrow stocked and armed with hunting tools and ready to go into action. Wow… does similar thing also happen in your culture? Do these cultures still exist? Before the hunting expedition, you will hear a lot of drumming and the blowing of local horns reminding people of where to meet and the time to meet; there were also appellations that make people wanting to join the adventure for the day. Those who had killed more of wild animals were always called first in that order. Could this be the reason why we have lost several animals to extinction? Today, appellations are given to people who have planted the most trees, who have conserved the extinct animals and protected the wetlands. I think that people should also be given appellations based on the one who wears the most weather friendly cloth, shoes, watches, and belts. May be people could be awarded since they drunk the most weather friendly water, soda, and smoke the most weather friendly cigar? And leaders of the world should also be taken seriously based on the weather friendly words and leadership styles and may be marriages be consummated based on a promise that not just for better for worst in the relationship but a promise to also protect the environment for better for worst. Scientist all over the world have been praised for their discoveries to protect the lives of the growing population. For instance, the medicine to fight Cancer, HIV, Ebola, Opioid and other addictions. All these efforts are geared towards improvement of the world. A healthy world is a wealthy world

WHY I LOVE THE BEAUTY OF THE ENVIRONMENT

Do you know why some people find happiness in their garden? And others find happiness in flowers? My environment, your environment and our environment can bring out that happiness. Why do you present beautiful flowers to someone you love? may be at the airport, during dating, weddings, or even during sad stories such as the lost of love ones? All these are indications that humans find love with the environment first before finding love with fellow humans. Humans have taken control of the environment to our benefits; think of the beautiful home with all the decorations, the schools with all the designs, the shopping malls with all the planning to make customers happy, think of the church and the mosque with the wonderful design to make worshippers happy and tune their worshippers mind towards the presence of God, think of the bridges, the cars, the trains, the aircraft, the ship in the water and how it moves, carrying cargo and people around the world. Some people find their healing in the environment such as the water they see at the river or the rocks they climb on the mountain. Others find their healing by looking at the birds flap their wings far away in the sky and making certain patterns of noise, others also find their joy by looking at the game cook, the horse race, the dog race, the bull ride. Have you ever seen the sea lion swim in the pool of water? Displaying its ability to speed swim? You may also find happiness in this wonderful animal. What of the trunk of the elephant and how this wonderful animal uses the trunk to pull down big trees, what of the beautiful display of the monkeys in the Madagascan forest? What of trekking the chimpanzees in the Ugandan forest and the rhinos in the Kenyan forest, you may want to think of a visit to the crocodile pond in Paga; the northern part of Ghana or the sanctuary park in Sunyani. A journey of no return in Cape Coast… the footprint of Naa Gbewa in Pusiga. A visit to the Crocodile pond will find some happiness by sitting on the back of these animals to take a selfie. What of a visit to the largest seaport in China or flying on the busiest airport in Atlanta or a visit to the falling bridge in London? Or may sitting on the canoe at the river Nile from Egypt to Uganda? Or may taking a cruise from Miami to Cuba? Have you ever thought of the design of the Christmas trees and the role it played around the world? It comes with happiness, memories and worship. The environment is our hope, it is our source of happiness and it is the source of our survival. Take a moment and ponder about the actions and in actions that may be harming the very source of your happiness, my happiness and our happiness and stand strong to protect the source of our happiness. What are we waiting for? Act now, powerful leaders of the world, what are you waiting for? Act now to save the environment, individuals lovers of the environment, what are you waiting for? Act now to save the environment, musicians of the of the world, actors and actress of the world, propagate the usefulness of the environment. Use your voice to educate us about the environment, what are we waiting for? John Mayer the musician once said that we might be waiting for the world to change. The world had changed because of our actions and in actions and will continue to change unless we change our actions and in actions towards the environment in a good way. Think of the virgin forest and the virgin land and their beauty, the joy, and the memories, man had exploited the virgin land, and the virgin forest to our advantage to the neglect of the very environment that provided us with our needs. On radio and other media channels, I have always heard of the glaciers and the melting ice, what will be our future if the ice melts and the earth is cover with water as a result of the heating of the atmosphere? Where do we go from here with this eminent threat? Let us not be waiting for the world to change but take action to change the world positively by stopping the extra heating. We should be worried that most people who are poor and may not be able to get a boat to float when the ice melt sending waves of water across the earth, we may not have life jacket to protect the entire family and love ones across the globe. Humans may suffer the consequence; our pets may suffer the consequence and the geography of the world may change, the way of worship may change, few lives may exist, leaving the earth hopeless, disappointed, and spiritless.

TAKING THE FUTURE OF THE ENVIRONMENT INTO OUR HANDS AND DOING THINGS THE RIGHT WAY

I will like to live in a very green environment, when I say green; I mean an environment with trees plenty of fresh air blowing. I like to admire flowers as they give a source of happiness, and I like to visit rivers that have stored water in them because water is life. It makes sense to say that tree planting should be taken seriously to protect the environment from the excessive heat; heat can cause rivers to dry up very quickly as a result of the evaporation of the water bodies. Excessive heat also causes the death of many water creatures such as the fish, the turtle, the shrimp, the whale, the crocodile, the sea lion, the frog, and all the other creatures in the water that do not want excessive heat. Planting trees along water bodies will help to prevent the migration and death of these creatures. However, there are a lot of problems associated with the planting of trees around the world; these trees need protection from other animals that prey on them, for instance, in many parts of Africa and other parts of the world where people believe in free ranch system where animals are allowed to grace freely; the associated problems are that the young plants mostly do not survive as a result of the gracing of animals. In most developed World such as the US, UK, Canada, Japan, and the EU Countries and other developed World, animals are controlled; making it easy for trees planted to grow without much difficulty. The culture of the free ranch system and the culture of closed ranch system are two faces of the coin that sometimes determine the survival of plans that support the environment. I was told by my science teacher that the presence of trees, mountains and rivers supports rain fall such as conventional, Orographic, Frontal, and Monsoonal rain fall. As humans as we are, we depend on the environment for our total survival; think of the water we drink, the food we eat, the air we breathe, are all from the environment. Polluting the environment means directing poisoning ourselves to death. Recall that plastic takes a long time to degrade, this means that any tiny pieces of plastics in our water system such as those dump knowingly and unknowingly after drinking our soda, energy drink, water and all the enjoyment drinks unfortunately found their way into the very sources of water we drink daily. One day, I was walking by a certain river, name withheld, and the plastics I saw in the river was very disgusting and very worrisome because I learn that river serves as the source of our drinking water. The river was so choked with plastic that I thought of my stomach as a plastic reservoir, because I am convinced that no amount of filtration can completely eliminate the plastics in the water we drink; no wonder we fall ill frequently and a lot of people dying all over the world as a result of water pollution. Our system is not able to break down the tiny plastics found in our drinking water, what a calamity?

....

....

....

....

....

....

....

....

....

....

....

....

....

....

Solving environmental issues are like the love of a flower that put a lot of smiles in the face of a love one or even people who are in sad moment find love with the flower. A holistic approach to the environmental issues are the best way to go; Government around the world, Companies around the world, Educators around the world, Scientist around the world and individuals around the world, your ideas, contributions and leadership styles are needed at this crucial time to solve the environmental issues for a better living.

ABOUT THE AUTHOR

Dr. Alhassan Ndekugri is currently a professor of Finance and International business. He had travel around the world on academic research and presentations. One interesting thing about Alhassan is that whiles traveling around the world by air, land and sea he observes the environment which is the motivation for writing this book. His education started in the small village of Baribari, northern part of Ghana and 5 kilometers away from the capital of Bawku in the Upper East Region of Ghana. Besides obtaining BS in Mathematics and Business from the University for Development Studies, Alhassan also obtained an MBA (Master of Business Administration) in Finance from the Notre Dame De Namur University in Belmont, California in 2014 and a Doctor of Business Administration in International Business from Argosy University, Tampa, Florida in 2017. Alhassan currently lives in Columbia South Carolina.